Our Old House

by Susan Vizurraga

illustrated by Leslie Baker

Henry Holt and Company · New York

Henry Holt and Company, Inc., *Publishers since 1866*, 115 West 18th Street, New York, New York 10011. Henry Holt is a registered trademark of Henry Holt and Company, Inc. Text copyright © 1997 by Susan Vizurraga. Illustrations copyright © 1997 by Leslie Baker. All rights reserved. Published in Canada by Fitzhenry & Whiteside Ltd., 195 Allstate Parkway, Markham, Ontario L3R 4T8. Library of Congress Cataloging-in-Publication Data: Vizurraga, Susan. Our old house / by Susan Vizurraga; illustrated by Leslie Baker. Summary: A girl living in an old house finds clues inside and out about its history and former occupants. [1. Dwellings—Fiction.] I. Baker, Leslie, ill. II. Title. PZ7.V850u 1997 [E]—dc20 96-44215 ISBN 0-8050-3911-2/First Edition—1997. Designed by Stephanie Saint Clair. Printed in the United States of America on acid-free paper. ∞ The artist used watercolor on Fabriano paper to create the illustrations for this book.

1 3 5 7 9 10 8 6 4 2

For Joseph, Christopher, and Annie,
who are growing up
in our old house
—S. V.

For Lance Brown,
whose sense of place and most magical design
transformed our old house into our much-loved home
—L. B.

There's a wisteria vine
that curls around
a post on our front porch.
It reaches to the rain gutter
and its blue flowers
look like a waterfall
spilling off the porch roof.

I like to lie on my back
and look up at that vine.
It's an old vine
and it's an old house.
It's our house now
but it hasn't always been ours.
It used to belong to someone else.

I know
because when Mom
pried the fireplace mantel
off the wall in the parlor
and turned it around
to clean the cobwebs from the back,
written on it was our address
in someone's old-fashioned handwriting
but the name written above it wasn't ours.
And when she scraped off the old paint,
Mom showed me the layers of color
that someone else had spread on our mantel
many years ago.

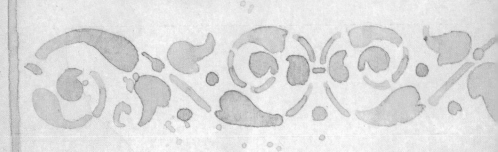

I know
there's a certain color to the roses
that grow in our neighborhood.
They're all daughters of the rosebush
outside our kitchen window.
I heard from the woman
who still lives next door
that the neighbors who lived on this street
when our rosebush was young
received a cutting, a little slip,
and each started to grow in a neighbor's yard.
All those roses have grown old together
and stayed where they were planted
while people moved in and out
of the houses on our street.

I know
that a different girl
once lived in our house.
Her name, *Ruth*,
is scratched, down low,
into the kitchen door
and the writing looks like a little girl's.
She must have been just learning to write
when she practiced on our door.
I wonder if her parents saw it there,
or maybe, besides Ruth,
I'm the only one who knows.

I know
some other children
once played in our yard.
When I helped Mom and Daddy
dig a straight, shallow path
for our new sidewalk,
I found a cracked glass marble
with a swirl of green inside.

I scrubbed off the dirt
and I keep that marble
in a treasure box on my dresser
with a small piece
of a brown thrasher's speckled egg
and a bracelet I made
from the colored glass beads
that I found in a secret place
beneath the loose front-porch step.

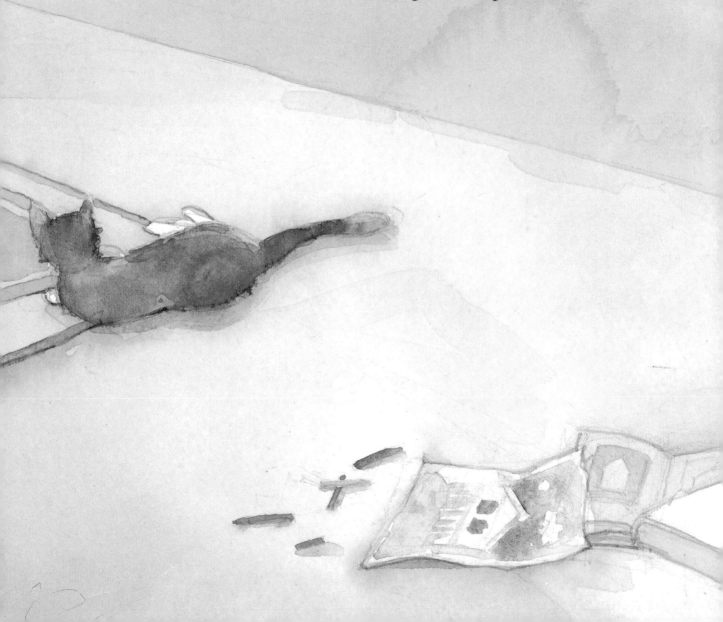

I know
someone once kept a garden
where our strawberries grow now.
When Daddy and I
pulled back the honeysuckle
and tucked it behind the old garden fence,
we found neat rows of raised earth
where someone else's vegetables used to grow.

And jonquils still open in the springtime
in a neat circle
around our wild cherry tree
but we aren't the ones who planted them there.
I know more about our house now.

When Daddy was patching the porch roof,
I was lying in the grass
and watching the wisteria
that's started tugging on the rain gutter.
I heard Daddy's voice
and I saw a woman
standing on that loose front-porch step
looking up at our old house.
I saw Daddy climb down the ladder
and brush off his hands.
He called to me
to come and meet the woman,
who sat on the porch swing
and looked all around
at the house and the yard.

"She used to live here," Daddy said,
and I leaned against a post
while I listened.
She talked about what a difference
a fresh coat of paint can make,
and how high
that vine had climbed
since she saw it last.
Daddy told her all about us
and the repairs we'd been making.

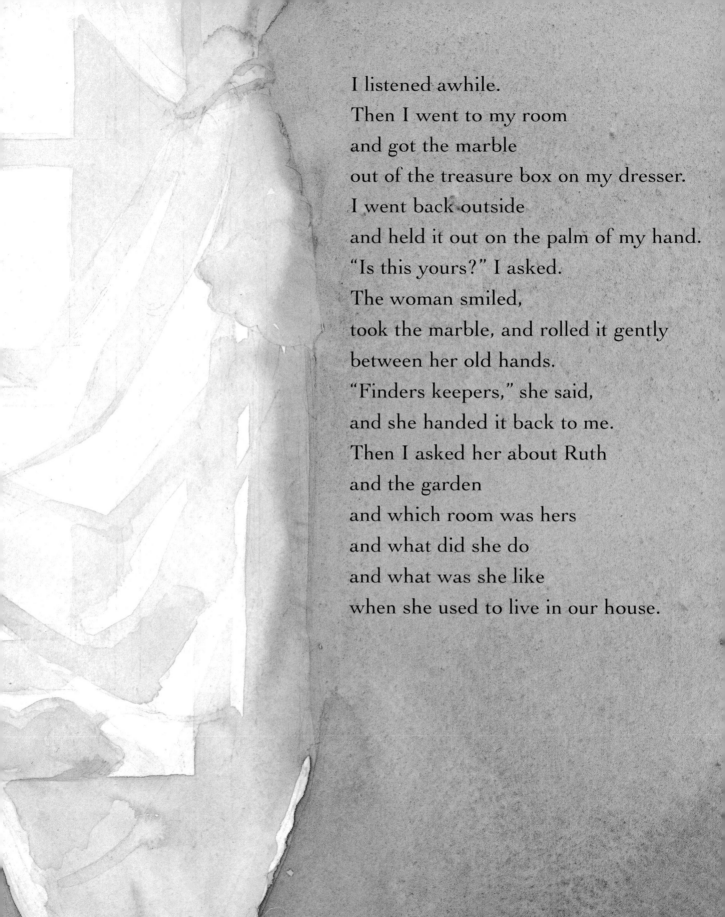

I listened awhile.
Then I went to my room
and got the marble
out of the treasure box on my dresser.
I went back outside
and held it out on the palm of my hand.
"Is this yours?" I asked.
The woman smiled,
took the marble, and rolled it gently
between her old hands.
"Finders keepers," she said,
and she handed it back to me.
Then I asked her about Ruth
and the garden
and which room was hers
and what did she do
and what was she like
when she used to live in our house.

After a while
the woman stood up
and clasped my hand in her right hand
and Daddy's in her left.
She looked back at us
on the porch of our house
as she walked away.

When she was gone
I took the box off my dresser
and I went out on the porch
and sat on the swing
and listened to Daddy
working on the roof above.
I took out my beaded bracelet
and tied it around my wrist
and I rolled the old marble
between my hands.
Then I put the marble
back in its place
among the other treasures
I've found around this house.
And I held the box
in my lap
and sat swinging on the front porch
for a long, long time.

When I am old,
that wisteria vine
may reach all the way to the chimney.
I may live in another house then,
and there may be someone else
who sits on our porch swing
and plays in our yard.
Someone who lies in the grass
and looks up at our wisteria vine.
Someone who finds the secret place
beneath the loose front-porch step.
Someone whose questions
I can answer.

So I hope someday
I, too, will return to visit
our old house.

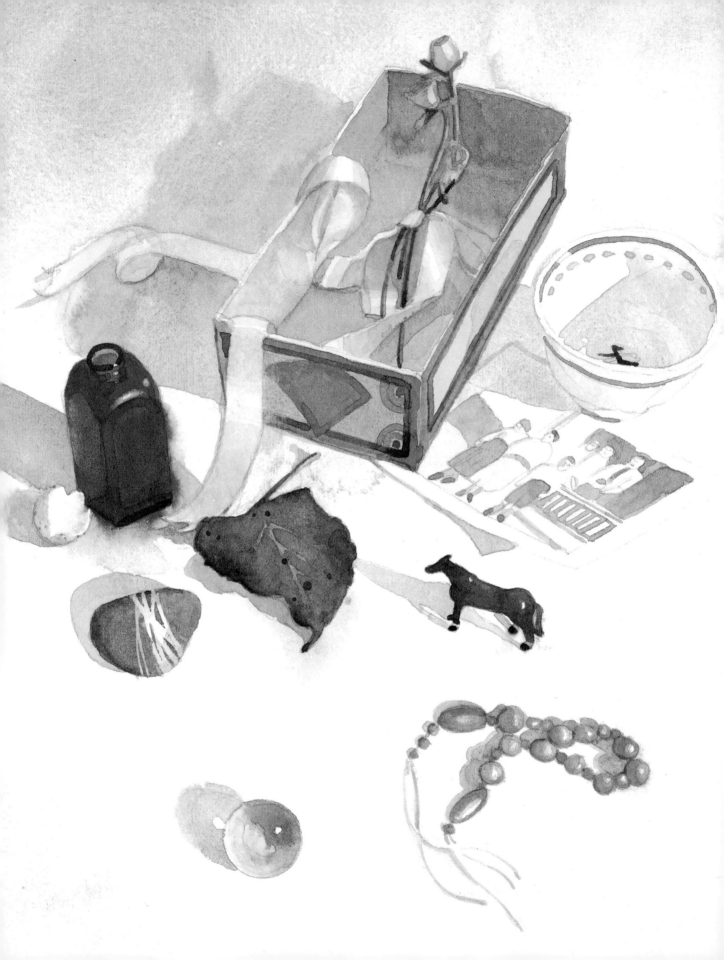